TOO MANY CHICKENS!

For Carol Kerr and Cheryl Dineen,

who inspire big and little writers

P. B.

For Esperanca

B. S.

First U.S. Edition 1991

First published in Canada by Kids Can Press Ltd.

ISBN 0-316-10358-6

Library of Congress Catalog Card Number 90-53441
Library of Congress Cataloging-in-Publication information is available.

Joy Street Books are published by Little, Brown and Company (Inc.)

10 9 8 7 6 5 4 3 2 1

Printed in Hong Kong by Wing King Tong Co. Ltd.

TOO MaNy CHICKENS!

Written by **Paulette Bourgeois**

Illustrated by **Bill Slavin**

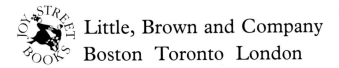
Little, Brown and Company
Boston Toronto London

Mrs. Kerr's class wiggled and squiggled and giggled. Farmer Berry had brought the eggs — a dozen eggs that would soon be chicks. They were oval and speckled and smelled like a chicken coop.

Michael Alexander wrinkled his nose. Mrs. Kerr rolled her eyes and asked Farmer Berry to put the eggs in the incubator.

The class took good care of the eggs. They turned them and checked them. They worried about them at night.

And then, on the twenty-first day, a crack marbled the surface of an egg. The crack widened.

"Rat, tat, tat," needled a beak.

For the very first time, Mrs. Kerr's class was still. The eggs opened, one by one, like ice cracking in the spring.

All the chicks hatched.
They were the color of
sweet butter and as soft
as cotton balls.

The principal came to see the chicks. Mr. Rufus, the custodian, came to see the chicks. Even the sixth graders came to see the chicks.

"Aren't they cute?" they cooed. The chicks went "Peep!" and tried to hop over the edge of the brooder.

On Monday, Farmer Berry was supposed to come and get the chicks, but she never arrived. By Thursday, the chicks were big enough to jump. Mrs. Kerr was worried.

Every day they grew a little bigger. They were
noisy and speckled and smelled like a chicken
coop. They roosted on the science table and
pecked under desks. They clawed at the carpet.
They took baths in the sinks and shook their soggy
feathers on the art supplies. They were always hun-
gry. Mrs. Kerr kept a bag of seed in her desk.

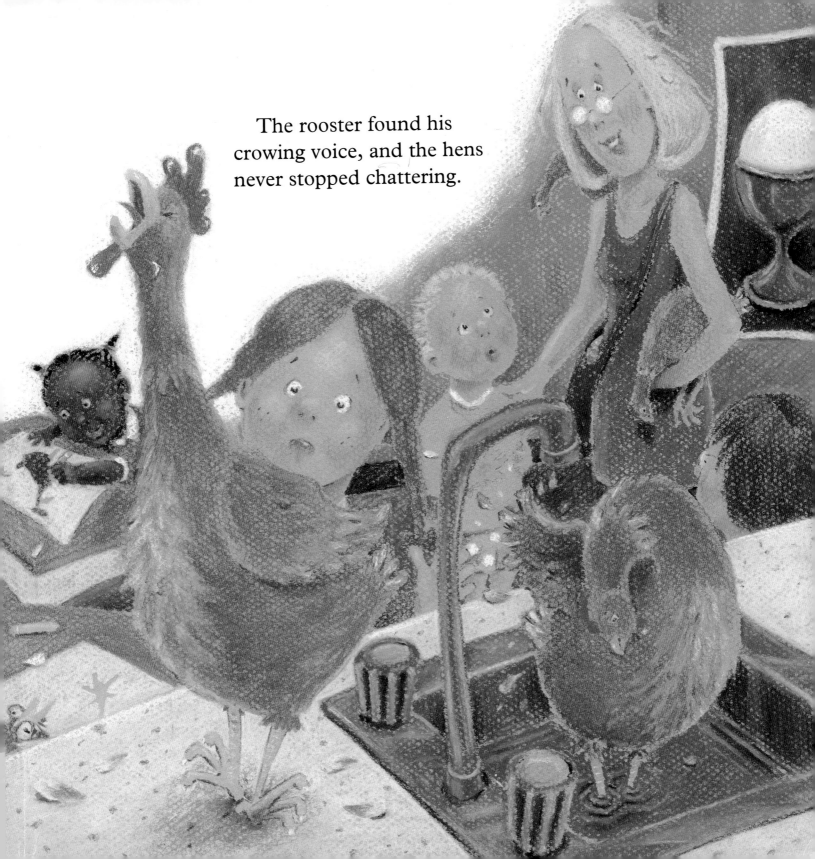

The rooster found his
crowing voice, and the hens
never stopped chattering.

"I CAN'T STAND THIS ANYMORE!" screamed Michael Alexander when a chicken walked across his brand-new notebook. "They are noisy and ugly and they stink!"

It was true. The chicks weren't cute anymore.
And they did smell. Nobody visited Room 17,
not even Mr. Rufus.

Then the hens started laying eggs.
Michael Alexander painted a sign, and Mrs. Kerr taught the children how to reach under the hens and gather eggs.

Finally, Farmer Berry came. She was very apologetic. She already had so many chickens she had forgotten to pick up the chicks. Farmer Berry looked around Room 17 and grinned.

"These chickens look so happy," she said. "I can't bear to take them away."

Before Mrs. Kerr could interrupt, Farmer Berry added, "Here's a little present for all you've done." Michael Alexander shuddered. Mrs. Kerr rolled her eyes.

"Bunnies," said Mrs. Kerr. "How cute."

The rabbits had long white fur, pink eyes, and crinkly wet noses.

The principal came to see the bunnies. Mr. Rufus came to see the bunnies. Even the sixth graders came to see the bunnies.

Soon, there were four more bunnies. Mrs. Kerr had to build a bigger cage. She kept carrots and alfalfa in her desk.

Before long, there were sixteen bunnies. But Mrs. Kerr wasn't worried. Michael Alexander painted a new sign, and Mrs. Kerr taught the class how to knit.

Soon everyone was wearing an angora hat. Even Farmer Berry. Why, she was so happy with her new hat that she gave Mrs. Kerr's class a present.

Michael Alexander gasped. Mrs. Kerr rolled her eyes. There, outside the school, hunched over the grass, was a great, big, old nanny goat.

"That old goat smells," said Michael Alexander.

"I know," said Mrs. Kerr.

"At least she eats the grass," said Michael Alexander.

"And I think Mr. Rufus likes her," said Mrs. Kerr.

The class didn't know what to do with the old goat. But Mrs. Kerr wasn't worried. Michael Alexander painted another sign. Mrs. Kerr kept apples in her desk and taught the children how to milk.

People liked the goat's milk. Mr. Rufus bought two glasses every morning and said he'd never felt better.

By now Mrs. Kerr's class had earned so much money from selling eggs and milk and hats, they decided to buy a small farm for the animals. And since Mr. Rufus liked his angora hat, goat's milk, and fresh eggs so much, he said he'd like to live there, too.

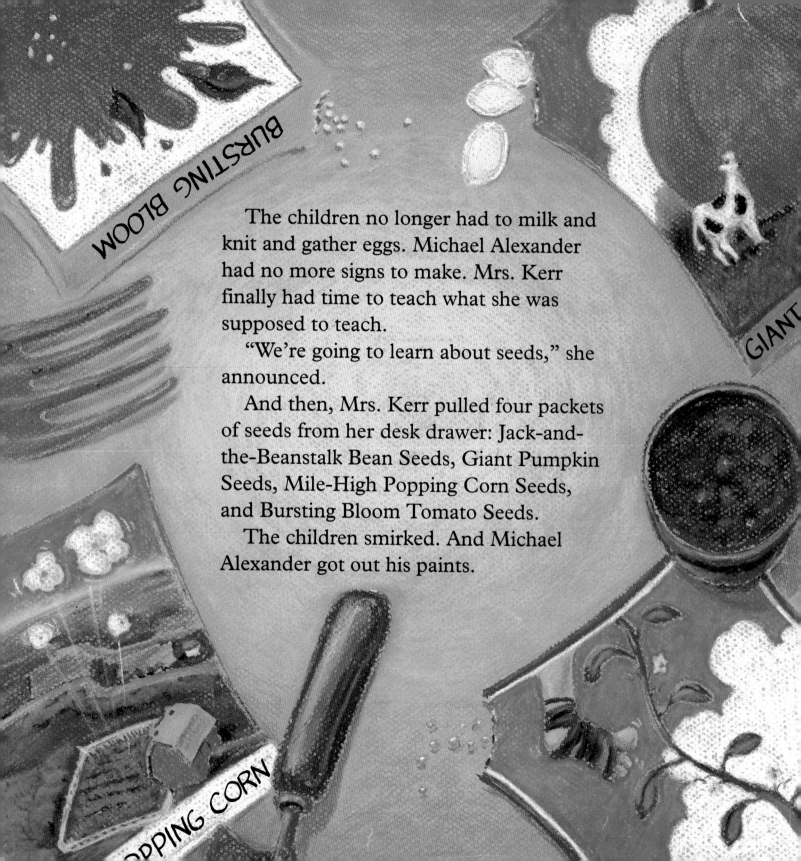

The children no longer had to milk and knit and gather eggs. Michael Alexander had no more signs to make. Mrs. Kerr finally had time to teach what she was supposed to teach.

"We're going to learn about seeds," she announced.

And then, Mrs. Kerr pulled four packets of seeds from her desk drawer: Jack-and-the-Beanstalk Bean Seeds, Giant Pumpkin Seeds, Mile-High Popping Corn Seeds, and Bursting Bloom Tomato Seeds.

The children smirked. And Michael Alexander got out his paints.

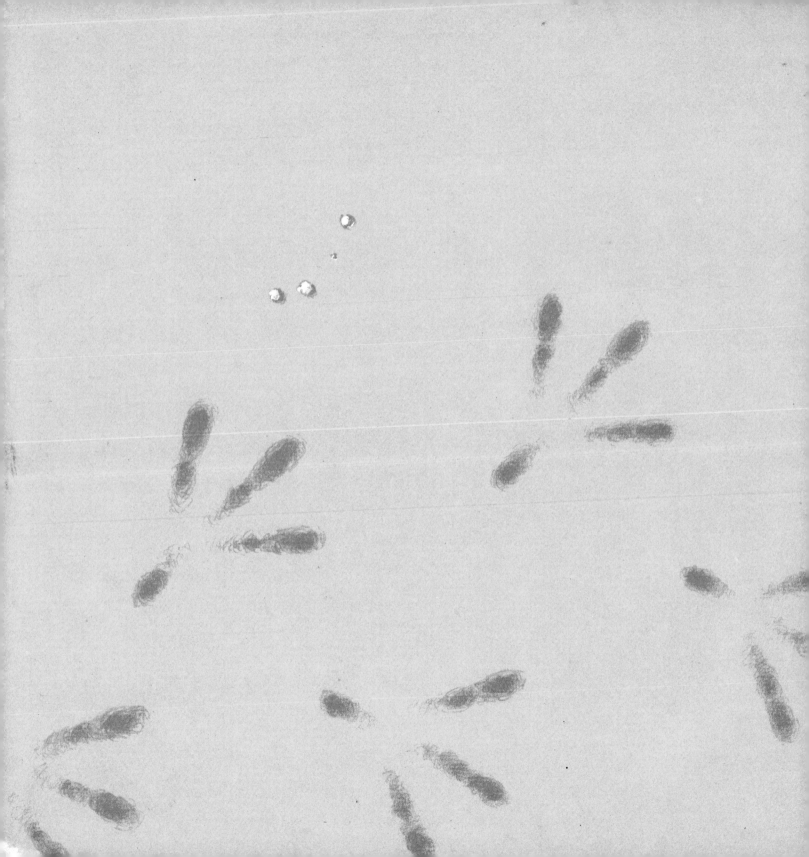